Accidental Resident

By

Ruby Dare

ACCIDENTAL RESIDENT

First edition. May 8, 2023.

ISBN: 979-8223708971

Written by Ruby Dare.

Table of Contents

~ Loc Isle ~

When some people change their lives, they change their hair, buy a new wardrobe and perhaps change their living situation or job. Tressa had done all of those things. Her last step was to travel. A once in a lifetime vacation before she started her new job. A twenty-one-day transatlantic cruise. She boarded the Starshine, a grandeur class ship from Sun-Star Cruises in New York City and would disembark in London. The ports of call along the way had really drawn her to this cruise, especially the city of Cork in Ireland.

Tressa woke early the day of their arrival in Cork. They would dock the ship from eight in the morning until four in the afternoon. She wished to spend as much time with feet on the ground as possible. Bag in hand, she impatiently waited to disembark the ship. She reviewed the contents of her pack one last time, making certain she had everything. Sketch pad, colored pencils, water, snacks, phone, cruise ID, and a photocopy of her passport. And the last minute decision of an extra pair of shorts and tee-shirt.

The balmy sun hit her long box braids, taking in the heat, warming her down to her scalp. It had been a great hairstyle choice for her long journey. They would stay looking fresh and wonderful for several months. She paid more to turn them two-toned. The streaks of copper especially glistened in the sunshine and water. A cool breeze made the warm summer day perfect. Tressa shifted her considerable weight from one leg to the other, gently swaying as she hummed to herself.

Finally, a crew member ushered her forward, scanning her cruise card before she could leave the ship. "Enjoy your stay in Cork. All tours are meeting to the right as you disembark. Please remember we leave at four sharp, so please be aboard before then."

"Thank you." She nodded to the attendant as she walked down the ramp and off the ship, tightening the sweatshirt around her waist. Tour guides watched as she passed all of them with their patrons, and hailed herself a taxi. She had other plans for the day.

The taxi dropped her off in Schull, and she rented a runabout. Then she headed out to Carbery's Hundred Isles. She looked to the sky, closing her eyes as she said a silent thank you to her dad for teaching her to drive boats so many years ago. It was a skill that stuck. She stopped at an island, seeing the remnants of an abandoned house. She secured her boat and grabbed her bag.

Tressa walked around the abandoned stone structure. Two walls and part of a chimney still stood. The door frame and steps up to the crumbling stone porch were intact. Stepping into the house, she began taking pictures and walking around. Grazing her fingers over the stone, she wondered who had built the house. It had likely been amazing in its heyday. Tressa wondered who the very first, as well as the very last, person to live in it had been like. Breathing deeply, she closed her eyes, imagining what it must have been like to bring the wood in, build up the fire to cook some stew over the flames, and bake homemade bread in the hearth.

Tressa stepped back outside and took several more pictures. The crumbling wall with the dilapidated remains of the chimney, called to her. It filled her with the warmth that comes with love and care, like family. She put down her towel by a tree, got out her sketchbook and colored pencils. Tressa felt her body relax as she started sketching. She loved the feel of each pencil. They were all different heights of sharpness, depending on how much her work favored one color over another. They became an extension of her mind, creativity, arm, and hand when she worked. It was all interconnected, what she saw in front of her, mixed with her own imagination.

Time flew by as Tressa sketched. She stopped occasionally, looking at what she had done, or taking some food and drink from her bag. Leaning against a tree, her eyes did a slow blink, and then another. Then they were closed for good. A light breeze tickled her face, but not enough to wake her. What did wake her was the sound of a horn. At first it was soft, weaving its way through her dreams, and then it got louder, interrupting a very passionate kiss with a man with piercing green eyes and soft curly hair. Someone she had never met.

Tressa awoke with a start, hearing the horn of her cruise ship. She swore as she checked her watch and gathered her things. Tressa had almost made it back to her roundabout. Only two more steps, and she would be aboard and on her way back to shore.

Fate had other plans. She tripped over a rock she didn't see. She landed on her knees as her bag went flying, falling on the edge of the far side of the runabout. It opened itself to the water. She watched as if in slow motion as the contents of her bag fell into the water and sank.

"No!" Tressa crawled to the boat and climbed aboard. Moving to her bag, she could grab it before it went overboard as well. The only thing left was her colored pencils and sketch book that had gotten stuck by the strap. She was able to scoop up her shorts and shirt. The photocopy of her passport was still floating. She grabbed it, happy to salvage such an important document, her only current form of ID, aside from her cruise card. The blood drained from her face as her heart started beating faster when she realized it was illegible. It was nothing but runny, washed out ink. Tressa's phone was nowhere in sight. She held down her fear as she started the roundabout and made her way back to shore.

Mac, the cabbie, was on his last fair of the day. He pulled into the boat rental parking lot. He always loved picking up fares from there. They were always nice, relaxed people, mostly tourists who were often generous tippers. He attributed it to his wonderful demeanor and accent.

Tressa hopped into his taxi. He didn't even have time to ask about her destination before she blurted. "The cruise ship dock please. Can you hurry? I'm late."

"Of course, lass." Mac nodded and heard out.

In the taxi, Tressa looked out the window as she tried to calm herself. She could make it. She was sure of that. And then she saw it. It knocked the air right out of her as her fear took hold. The ship was moving! It was moving away, and she was not on it. She could feel her body shake slightly, her palms sweating. She could feel her chest tighten, and she was having trouble breathing.

"Are you alright ma'am?" Mac looked in the rear-view mirror. "Would you like some water?" He reached back to hand her a bottle of water.

Tressa took the water as she gave the driver a once over. He had caring eyes. He looked like she was genuinely concerned for her. Tressa wondered if he dealt with a lot of tourists in distress or was just a really kind man. "I missed my ship," she whispered, tears welling in her eyes, that she wouldn't dare let fall.

"What was that?" The cabbie's brows furrowed with worry.

"I - I missed my ship. I was on a cruise, I took too long on shore, I fell asleep, and now I've missed my ship." With that, Tressa could no longer hold back the flood of tears as she became a blubbering mess. Her cries turned to hiccups.

"Sounds like you need a drink, ma'am."

"Please, call me Tressa. I think I need to go to the police or something."

"They can't help you, trust me." Mac turned his cab around and headed back to town.

Tressa was at the mercy of the cab driver. A sense of relief and calm washed over her as her hiccups subsided. She still wasn't sure of her options, but Mac's voice was very soothing.

Mac dropped her off in front of O'Rourkes Pub. "Now, lass, you head on inside. Get yourself a drink and a meal. And ask for Callum. You tell him Mac sent you. The meal's on me, and he'll help you with your troubles."

"Are you sure?"

"No truer words have I ever said. Now off with you, young lass."

Tressa couldn't help but laugh. She was not a young lass. At thirty-two, her life had crashed and burned, and now she was building it back from the ground up. The cruise was supposed to be her time to recharge so she could rise from the ashes like a phoenix and figure out her next move. "Thank you." Tressa reached for the cash in her pocket.

Mac raised his hand, waving her off. "No, no, this one's on me. You need to save what little precious money you have."

Tressa realized he was right. Aside from the extra T-shirt and pair of shorts, she had no clothes except what was on her back. Her money was almost nonexistent as the bulk of her cash and all her credit cards were in the safe in her cabin. She now had no ID other than her cruise card in her back pocket, and no phone. She racked her brain to see whose phone numbers she had memorized.

Tressa gave Mac a heartfelt smile. "Thank you, I appreciate that. I'll pay you back when I can."

Mac smiled back. "Think nothing of it. I would hope someone would do the same for my daughter in a jam. Now, off you go. And remember to ask for Callum."

Tressa nodded as she gathered her bag and got out of the taxi. She waved as Mac pulled away. She wiped her eyes, squared her shoulders and headed towards the pub's front door.

~ O'Rourke's Pub ~

Callum O'Rourke stood behind the bar of his pub. Tall and toned, his powerful arm covered the bar with two swipes as he wiped it down. He moved a fallen dark curl behind his ear. All the while, he kept a watchful eye on a town regular sitting at the opposite end. The season was in high gear and he needed more help. Aside from a couple more servers, he was even considering hiring a part-time bouncer. He was tired of dealing with the drunks like the one sitting at the end of the bar. He gave a slight smirk as he thought about how nice it would be to let someone else duck the punches, even though it didn't happen too often.

Sighing, he strolled over to Roland, the regular at the end of the bar. Callum pulled the empty beer mug away from the inebriated gentleman in front of him. "Sorry, but that's your last one. Time to go."

"Says who?" Roland slammed his hand on the bar. He wasn't ready to stop drinking. And Callum should just let him be. He wasn't bothering anyone, well, except the server he wanted to date. Eventually, she would say yes. "I'm a patron. You're the bartender, so tend the bar and pour me another beer."

Callum had enough. One of his servers had already complained about Roland. He needed to keep the people that worked for him safe. What kind of man would he be if he didn't stand by the side of the ladies he employed? "You're locked, mate. I said it's time to go."

"Piss off, I'm not your mate. Ya can't make me leave."

"Fine, you're not my mate, but this *is* my pub. See, that's my name outside, so if I say it's time to go, then it's time to go. Don't make me throw you out."

Roland looked at Callum and sneered. They had never been friends and never would be. But Callum had the best pub in town and Roland didn't want to get permanently banned. So he just shrugged, threw some money on the bar and stormed towards the door.

Callum shook his head and took the money. "Damn day drinkers."

As Roland was leaving, he knocked over the woman entering, sending her to the floor.

"Excuse you!" Tressa yelled at the asshole who ran into her.

Roland turned, giving her one of his best sneers, before walking all the way out.

Callum hopped over the bar, ready to help the newcomer up. "I know I run a terrific place, but you didn't have to fall in love so literally," He chuckled. "I'm Callum O'Rourke and this is my pub." He held out his hand to her. "Are you alright?"

Calum was stunned by the women on the floor. Her ebony skin glowed. He took in her curves and rolls. They were beautiful to him. Finally, her big, chocolate brown eyes sucked him into a euphoria like state. She had a sense of familiarity with him, yet he was sure he did not know who she was. Finally, he was able to speak. "And who might you be?"

Tressa looked up at the man, extending a hand to her. He was strong and had the most intense green eyes she had ever seen. It took her breath away, leaving her with no words. The curl tucked behind his ear fell as it lightly caressed his face before landing over his eye. Her stomach fluttered as she thought about the curls she had run her hands through in her dream. They looked the same. She wanted to reach out and see if they felt the same, but she resisted the urge.

Tressa took the help in getting up. Taking his hand, she felt a shock move through her body, ending in her stomach, making it flutter like butterflies. Once up, she quickly removed her hand from his.

"I - I'm Tressa." She stretched her back a little and wiped her hands over her ass, removing a small amount of floor dust.

Callum took her gently by the arm. "Here, have a seat." He guided her to a chair at an empty table. "And I'll get you some water." Sitting Tressa in the chair, he walked to the bar, getting her some water.

At the table next to her was a couple who looked a little too comfortable to be mere tourists. They looked to be about in their sixties. Both with silver peppered in their hair. Helen and her husband, Pat, came in twice a week to have lunch at O'Rourkes. They were Callum's favorite regulars. They had seen the entire altercation. Helen seemed concerned. Her motherly instincts were kicking in.

"Are you okay, dear? You took quite the tumble when you came in. My name is Helen. Come, sit with us." The man next to her introduced himself. "I'm Pat." He pulled out an empty chair for Tressa to sit in. "Please, sit."

Tressa smiled, thinking of her grandparents. Their passing had been hard on her. She was getting a little taste of having them back with Helen and Pat. She relished in the comfort and ease she felt in their presence, so she took the seat that was offered.

"Do you need some help, dear? You look a little frazzled. And not just because of yer tumble," Pat observed.

Tressa felt her tears well up again. She gulped several times to push them back down. "I was out on one of the Carbery's Hundred Isles, and I fell asleep, and I missed my ship! What the hell am I gonna do?"

The silver-haired woman took her hand and gave it a reassuring pat. "Did you fall asleep out there, lass?"

Tressa thought it was an odd question coming from Helen. "Yes, that's why I missed my ship. I just said that!"

"Ah! Then you missed the ship on purpose. It was the will of the isle." Helen clapped her hands.

"What?" Tressa was beyond confused.

"When you fall asleep out there, did you dream too?" Pat questioned.

"I - Of course I always dream." She looked from Helen to Pat. They were beaming. This was pointless. She needed to find Callum and, if not him, maybe Mac. He would help her again.

"Perhaps you dreamt of a man? A handsome stranger?" Helen was almost as giddy as a schoolgirl gossiping about a cute boy.

Tressa looked at Helen and Pat. They were leaning in, curious about what she would say. They were so interested in her dreams they had no thoughts of helping her. "What? Why does that matter?"

Helen laughed. "She did! Look at her face! But she doesn't want to tell us."

"See, lass, there is a legend that whoever falls asleep on the Isle of Locs will dream of their true love and become fated to meet them. Because from that moment on, their heart is now locked to their love."

Tressa shook her head. "But it was on Carbery's Hundred Isles. Not Loc Isle or whatever you called it."

"Correction, miss, that is what the collection of the islands are called. But most have their own names. But only three carry the legend. I'm surprised you didn't see anyone else dozing out there. That's how I met my love." Pat squeezed Helen's hand and gave it a kiss.

"There's the one with the broken-down house. The one with the upside-down boat with a hole in the hull." Helen put two fingers up.

"Oh, yes, the one with the broken oar! That's a good one! That's where I took the best snooze of my life that led me to you." Pat chuckled.

Helen blushed. "And last, but not least, the one with the little hill that is covered in clovers."

Tressa realized she had been on the one with the house. She shook her head. It was a legend, a silly superstition, it didn't matter to her. She needed to figure out how to get home. "This is very interesting, but I need some help."

"Now, now, you two, are you regaling this poor lady with tales of fiction?" Callum walked over with a tray of water, beer, and a bowl of what looked like a thick stew and a chunk of sourdough bread on the side. He placed it in front of Tressa.

She smiled, grateful for the food and drink. She took a couple of bites. The stew was beyond delicious. She leaned back in her chair, relaxing and taking a moment to enjoy the delicacy in her mouth. "Oh my, this is amazing. Thank you so much. "

Callum smiled. He was proud of his cooking abilities; he had a very Irish grandmother who taught him everything he knew about the kitchen t. She was the one to thank for his delicious menus.

When Tressa's brain settled, she realized something. "Wait, you introduced yourself as Callum. You are who I'm looking for! Mac said you could help me."

The smile on Callum's face disappeared and turned into a scowl.

"Damn that Mac! Keeps treating me like I'm the pied piper of helpless women and damsels in distress. I help one, maybe two ladies, and now I'm the town's charity." Callum had meant to say that under his breath, but he had gotten loud, allowing Tressa to hear every word.

Tressa pushed her chair back and grabbed her bag. "Well, I can see the Irish hospitality stopped with Mac. I'm not a damsel in distress. I can get along fine without your so-called charity." Tressa stood, ready to head for the door.

Callum felt terrible. Although those were his true feelings, he had not meant to be so harsh with her. "Wait! At least sit and have a meal and drink. If Mac sent you, I know he's paying for this." He shrugged. She was vexing, yet there was something that made it impossible for him to take his eyes off her.

Tressa turned and looked at Callum. Although she disliked the man standing there, she was hungry. She'd only had a few snacks on the Isle. And with the stressful morning, she'd worked up an appetite. The first two bites she had taken were divine.

Although she would never let Callum know, she headed back to the table, making a large circle to avoid him.

Tressa looked at him as she made the wide circle. She got a catch in her throat when she realized he *was* the man she had kissed in her dreams. Why hadn't she seen it before? Maybe because it was hidden by his curly hair that she just wanted to twirl her fingers around. Or maybe because she was having a crazy day, but there it was, plain as day. A four-leaf clover tattoo behind his left ear, just like in her dream. She scoffed. Now she knew the legend couldn't be true. There was no way she'd ever kiss the likes of Callum O'Rourke.

Tressa sat and started eating again. Callum pulled up a chair next to her. If Mac sent her, he had to help. He watched her a moment before speaking, letting her get some nourishment in her belly. "You need to go to the embassy."

"I know that!" Tressa snapped as she pulled a piece of sourdough off and dipped it in her stew. Her face grew hot with embarrassment. The embassy had never occurred to her. Why hadn't she read through the "Leaving Port Reminders" brochure the cruise ship had given her? She wouldn't be in this jam if she'd been better prepared. She was kicking herself for her blasé attitude. "I'm sorry for snapping. Especially since you are just trying to help." She took a swig of her beer. It, too, was the best beer she had ever had. She would have to remember the brand. Tressa hoped it wasn't one that was only available in Ireland. "But I don't know where it is here."

"It's in Dublin. A short three -ish hour drive depending on traffic. Unless you take the bus. Then it's more like twelve to fifteen hours with all the stops." Helen confirmed.

"Fifteen hour bus ride?" Tressa sighed. She was not looking forward to that. Maybe she could get in touch with her best friend, Marta, and she could front her the money for a plane ticket. Then she could just leave from Cork. No. She'd still need help from the embassy getting an ID and passport to travel out of the country. Tressa knew she didn't even have enough money for the bus fare, let alone getting duplicates of official documents.

"Don't look so forlorn, Miss Tressa. I'll help you. Mac gave you his word that I would help you. And that's a word I can't and won't break." He put his hand on her shoulder and gave it a reassuring squeeze.

Tressa looked at Callum. For the first time, she had a glimmer of hope. But with his next words, hope turned to dread.

"Unfortunately, the embassy is closed for the next four or five days. Some structural damages occurred. Bad flooding last month due to some storms was left unchecked." Callum explained.

"And now they just need to bulk the place up before they let all the bigwigs back to their offices." Pat chimed in.

"Five day paid vacation for all involved, really." Helen laughed.

"Five days?! What am I supposed to do for five days? I have no money, no clothes, and no place to stay." The events of the day were taking a toll on Tressa. She closed her eyes, taking several deep breaths.

Callum sighed. Regretting what he was about to say, he said it, anyway. "I've got a spare room above the bar. It's nothing special, but it's clean and comfortable. You are welcome to it. Also, if you want some cash, I can use a server in the pub in the afternoons. Business is picking up, especially with all the cruise ships docking. "

Tressa's eyes narrowed. Was he making a dig? Making fun of her situation? She crossed her arms, biting her tongue. She needed to hear him out.

"I'm down a server and we are getting busy. In five days' time, I'll drive you to the embassy myself. Get you all squared away." Callum liked the idea of having Tressa around for a few more days. Maybe he could get to know her. Maybe she would stop being vexing and just be hot and intriguing.

Tressa relaxed her arms a bit as she thought about the situation. Did she have a choice? It was a chance to make some money. This could work out. She just needed to roll with whatever came her way. And right now, she needed to roll with this unusual circumstance and opportunity.

Tressa knew she had to take Callum's offer, even though she didn't want to be in such proximity to him. Or did she? Why was she resisting him so much? He clearly had something that made her palms sweat and her heartbeat a little faster. But that wasn't always a good thing. And she really didn't know him. All she knew was that he was a handsome pub owner who was showing a stranger some kindness.

Did he live above the bar too? She assumed he did. Maybe it was just a rental space, and he lived far from the bar. Yes, and she would only have to see him at work. And in all honesty, she had no choice. Besides, it would only be a short time. The embassy would reopen in days, not weeks, and it would give her a chance to explore Cork. "Thank you for the offer, Mr. O'Rourke. I accept, and I appreciate the help."

"Aye! It's Callum, please. Mr. O'Rourke is my father. "

A small smile spread across Tressa's lips. "Alright, Callum."

~ Upstairs at Callum's ~

Callum clapped his hands, running them together. "Great! Let me show you the room before I put you to work."

"Hold on, you want me to start today? Now? Can I at least catch my breath? Try to contact the ship? Buy some damn clothes?!"

"Why do you want to contact the ship? It's not like they'll be coming back for you." Callum snorted.

"Maybe because I'm supposed to be on board, and they should know I'm not. Or, I don't know, call me crazy, but I'd like to get my shit back!" She threw her hands up in the air. This was going to be harder than she had hoped.

"I'm pretty sure they already know. Cruise Lines are pretty good with that kind of thing." Callum snorted as he crossed his arms. "Are you always so hostile and prickly? Well, princess. Let me show you to your quarters and then, when you feel like gracing the pub with your presence, you can work." Callum turned, not giving her a moment to respond. Instead, he just raised his hand, snaking his index finger with a come hither movement. "Any day now, princess prickly."

Tressa could feel the anger rising in her. Who the hell did this guy think he was? Yes, she needed his help. But was he always going to be an ass? But she was stuck, and she knew it.

Swallowing her anger, she took a deep breath and then followed the beckoning finger.

The stairs were steep and uneven, and there were a lot of them. They creaked with every step Tressa took. Callum's long legs had no problem bounding up each step. She envied his fluidity. Tressa could hold her own, but she would need to get used to the unpredictability of each step before she was fluid, like the man leading her. It gave her a chance to look at his ass. Small but muscular, fitting his tall form well. She wondered if either cheek had dimples, but either way, they were very biteable. She shook the thought from her head as she reached the landing.

For the second floor of a pub, it surprised her how many windows it had, allowing so much sunlight to shine through. She suspected moonlight would do the same and look beautiful as it shone against the wood and light sconces. At some point, she would want to draw that. She followed Callum halfway down the hall.

He stopped in front of a door. He opened it, then moved aside to let Tressa in. When she walked past him, he couldn't help but inhale her scent. He wasn't sure if it was her perfume, or shampoo, or just her natural smell, but it was intoxicating. He breathed deeply, praying she wouldn't notice while cursing himself for finding himself attracted to *his* prickly princess. His eyes sprung open, realizing his thoughts. For a brief second, he had thought of Tressa as his. He would be glad when the Embassy reopened.

"It's not much, but it's clean and comfortable. The bathroom is across the hall from your room. There is a linen closet next to it. Should have everything you need. Why don't you get settled, relax, do whatever. Come on down when you get hungry. I include meals with the gig." With that, Callum nodded and closed the door behind him.

Callum stood in the hall, running his hand through his curls. He took a deep breath in and let it out. What the hell had he gotten himself into with this one? She was both vexing, yet tantalizing at the same time. Both things he wanted no part of. He made a mental note to have a chat with Mac. His pied piper days were officially over. Callum went back downstairs. He had a pub to run.

~ **Little Sister** ~

Tressa put her bag on the bed. She walked to the window, opening the curtains and then the window. She smiled, seeing the curtains in the room. There was a dresser with a mirror, full-size bed and a radio on the nightstand. She sat on the bed, surprised at how comfortable it was. Tressa emptied the contents of her bag on the bed. She checked the inner pockets just to make sure she had missed no other cash she may have stashed on a previous use. There was nothing. She shook her head, again chastising herself for being so stupid in her packing, but relieved she had at least brought an extra shirt and shorts. Although that wouldn't help her with something to sleep in, or clean underwear for the next day. Any other time she would have picked up her phone and Googled a place to buy some basics. But her phone was at the bottom of the Isles somewhere.

Tressa needed to bite the bullet and ask Callum for a place to get some essentials. Maybe if Helen and Pat were still downstairs, she could just ask them and avoid Callum all together. Tressa made her way down the stairs, looking to see if she could spot Callum before he spotted her. So far, her plan was working. That was until she crashed into a woman coming out of the double-door kitchen with a basket of wings and a plate of loaded potato skins.

Tressa tried to avoid the server moving at warp speed. But she was clearly a woman on a mission and was moving too fast. Tressa could see her try to dodge her as she rolled her body, only bumping hips with Tressa as she came off the last step.

"Whoa there, didn't realize we needed a stop light here."

"I am so sorry! I didn't see you." Tressa moved out of the way.

Maggie laughed. "I can see that. Excuse me, I need to make this delivery."

"Uh, are Helen and Pat still here?" Tressa was sure the server would know who they were.

"Got their check in my pocket." Maggie slapped her left hip, revealing a server receipt holder in her back pocket.

"I can give it to them if you would like." Tressa reached for Maggie's back pocket.

Maggie swiped her ass around like she was doing a country line dance. "Sorry, but I don't know you from the leprechaun under the bridge. I'll be giving it to them in a minute if you stop holding me up."

Tressa felt insulted, but in the same position, she wouldn't have let a stranger take a receipt to the guest, either. "I'm Tressa. I'm the new server, I guess."

"You guess? Guesses are like wishes, just because you say it, doesn't make it so."

Callum walked over before Tressa could say anything else.

"Mags, I see you've met the prickly princess."

Tressa crossed her arms, ready to dispute her horrible new nickname.

Callum winked, disarming her. "This is Tressa. She'll be helping us for the week. I need you to show her the ropes tomorrow." He looked Tressa up and down. "She says she has things she needs to do today."

Tressa's blood boiled. He made her sound lazy or entitled, and she was neither. She turned to Maggie. "I got stuck here, missed my ship. So I need some clothes and things."

Maggie shoved her tray at Callum. "These are for table five." Turning back to Tressa, she wrapped her up in a hug. "Oh, you poor dear! I know where you can get what you need. I'll take you myself."

"Not until after your shift, Mags."

Maggie put her hands on her hips. "Um, table five won't wait forever."

"I - you -" Callum's face began turning beat red. "It is my name outside the pub, is it not?"

Maggie gave Callum a wink. "Best boss ever."

Callum shut his mouth, not wanting to say something he would regret. He just wanted this day to end.

Maggie grabbed Tressa's hand. "Come on, I know where to go. And I'm Maggie, by the way."

Callum gave the food to table five just as Maggie, and Tressa headed for the front door. "Mags! What are you doing to me? You can't leave now!"

"Sorry, but my new bestie needs some clothes. Poor girl is a train wreck. Just look at her."

Callum looked Tressa up and down. Train wreck, yes, but a beautiful one. "You could just tell princess prickly here, where to go. In fact. I'll give my old pal Mac a call and he can drive. He owes me."

"Callum O'Rourke! Is that any way to treat our guest? Your grandma would be ashamed! Don't make me call her and tell her." Maggie gave Tressa a wink. She had played Callum's weakness. There was no way he would say no now.

Callum's face started turning red again. It amused Tressa as she watched the blush creep up his neck until it was at the tip of his head. "Fine! One hour only! I'm serious, Mags. You're my best, and I need you here."

Maggie kissed Callum's cheek. "I'll stay late tonight, promise." She felt a little guilty about leaving him in the lurch, but it was slow at the moment and, as the spoiled little sister she was, she knew he would forgive her. And she'd make it up to him. "Have I ever told you what a wonderful boss you are?"

Callum rolled his eyes. "One hour Mags."

Maggie undid her apron and threw it at Callum. Reaching over the bar, she grabbed her purse. "Got it, two hours tops. Thanks, boss!" She smiled and grabbed Tressa by the hand, dragging her out of the pub.

"Dammit!" Callum said, a little louder than he thought.

"Come over, Cal, have a seat for a moment." Helen waved him over.

Callum sat down, exasperated. "Now I'm down two servers. Hell, I don't even know if princess prickly knows how to serve!"

Helen couldn't help but chuckle. "Oh, Callum, you've got it bad."

"That was pretty quick," Pat nodded.

"What are you two talking about? I've got what bad? The lack of help in my pub? Yes, yes. I've got that in spades."

"Oh, you poor deluded boy. You like Tressa." Helen smiled.

Callum stood up. "I'm cutting you both off. You've clearly had way too much to drink."

"Been out on any of the Isles, have you, Cal?" Pat called after him, giving a mischievous laugh.

Callum turned, ready to school Pat and Helen on a thing or two. Instead, he just stared at them as they smiled back at him. Was he that obvious? Could they really tell that he actually likes princess prickly? He shook his head at no one in particular. The idea was beyond ridiculous. He pointed at the two of them. "Cut off, I tell ya!" He turned and walked behind the bar.

~ McGreggor's ~

Maggie took Tressa to her favorite department store, McGreggor's. Although Tressa was quite a bit larger than she was, Maggie knew they would find some trendy clothes in the larger size that Tressa needed. No grandma looks for her. Once inside, Maggie looked around for a plus size section. She herself always shopped in the misses.

Tired of being dragged around, Tressa headed for the makeup counter. "Excuse me-"

"Well, hello there. May I interest you in a new lipstick? We have a wonderful shade of rustic mahogany that would look great against your skin tone. And it has a built-in moisturizer." She looked at Tressa's lips.

Tressa pursed her lips, aware of how incredibly chapped they were. Before she knew it, the attendant was placing a sample of lipstick in her hands. "Here, try it." She paced a mirror in front of Tressa.

Tressa looked for Maggie, but another associate had absconded with her to a makeup counter down the aisle. Sighing, she thought that if she played along, she would get the information she had come for. Tressa took the sample and tried it. It felt soothing and cool on her lips. She could feel her lips soaking in the built-in moisturizer. She rubbed her lips together, letting the color absorb and spread out a bit. Staring in the mirror, she looked at her lips and puckered. The attendant was right. The shade looked wonderful on her. She couldn't help but smile. It somehow made her feel bold and sexy. Feelings she hadn't felt in a while: feelings she was hoping the cruise would restore. Who knew a department store in Ireland was all she needed? "What's this called?"

"It's called *Deep Desire*. It looks lovely on you." The attendant smiled.

Tressa paused for a moment, debating. It would probably take the last of her cash. But as a woman who was big on retail therapy, she knew it would make her feel better. Feel more like herself when she wasn't in crisis mode.

The attendant could see the hesitation on her face. "It's on sale. Sixty percent off. For some reason, it's not selling well." The attendant looked around and lowered her voice. "Please don't tell anyone I said that."

Tressa could tell she meant it. "I'll take two, please. Not being from here, I don't want to run out too soon."

"Ah! The accent gave it away." The attendant rang her up, throwing in several extra samples of the same shade and two other shades in the bag. "Gotta keep you stocked." She gave Tressa a wink.

Tressa smiled. "Thank you so much. Oh, can you tell me where the plus size department is?"

"Go up the escalator two floors. Then, take a right as you're getting off, and it'll be at the back."

The smile left Tressa's face. Another store hiding away their plus size clothes like it was a dirty secret.

The attendant, a little on the large side herself, nodded a silent solidarity. "I know, but it's a fantastic selection. I promise you won't walk out of here looking like great aunt Gertrude." She gave Tressa's hand a gentle squeeze. "Come back if you need help."

Tressa's smile returned. She loved meeting kind strangers. It helped her keep her faith in humanity. "Thank you so much. I hope you have a wonderful rest of your day."

"You as well, Miss."

Tressa nodded and went off to find Maggie and together they headed to the secret floor of shame.

Two hours later, Maggie and Tressa came through the pub door, multiple packages in hand, laughing.

"Well, fuck all Mags! I said one hour. That's sixty minutes! You left and thirty minutes later, I was in the weeds. I'm docking your pay, and there will be no tip sharing for you today!"

Maybe it was because of the day she was having, or the lovely store attendant who helped bring back a piece of her inner fire. Whatever it was, Tressa couldn't see the one person who had made her feel like she could actually have an enjoyable time in Cork get penalized for helping her. Dropping her bags, she marched right up to Callum and looked him in the eye. "Why the hell are you so mean? She was just trying to help me. To be nice and comforting. Much like Mac and Pat and Helen. And then there is you! Don't be the asshole pub owner!" Tressa was panting, her anger rising from her toes. She was so close to him. He smelled like cedar and honey, distracting her from her anger for a moment.

Callum looked down at her, listening to her overreact. His height was a significant advantage at this moment. He felt torn between tearing her a new asshole and kissing her. She was so close. She smelled like sea air and vanilla. How could she smell so wonderful after the day she had had? It was dinnertime at this point. And why did he care? She was single-handedly ruining his business for the day. Would it be like this until she left? Callum looked around the pub. There were maybe twelve patrons at tables and three or four at the bar. Most of them were local, only a couple were tourists.

"Alright! That's it! Mags, get your ass in an apron and get back to work! We'll discuss your tips later." No one moved. They were all just staring at him. He clapped his hands over his head. "Chop chop! Get moving!!"

Maggie felt bad for Callum's outburst and for Tressa, knowing it was partially her fault. She quickly grabbed an apron and started working. Maggie had heard him use his 'boss voice' only a handful of times. She knew better than to challenge him.

Callum grabbed Tressa by the arm. "Not you Princess Prickly. You and I will have a chat. And by chat, I mean I'll do the talking, and you'll do the listening." He walked her to his office in the back and pulled out the chair in front of his desk. "Sit here, don't move. I'll be right back."

Tressa was stunned, angry, insulted, and a little turned on. All of which made her very uncomfortable. Tressa could hear Callum's shoes as he walked back towards the office. He put a plate of food and a glass of wine in front of her. Then he walked around to the other side of the desk and sat down.

"I don't want to be the asshole pub owner." He took a sip of his wine and pointed to Tressa's glass. "You seem like you might be a wine kind of woman."

Part of her wanted to feel insulted, that he would assume. But a greater part of her liked he could read people. It must come in handy in his line of work. She nodded.

"I'm going to guess further and say a syrah." He didn't wait for her to respond. As he nudged the glass a little closer to her. "Eat. I thought you might be hungry after all of that shopping. It's not poisoned, I promise."

Tressa smirked. "Poison is usually a woman's game. I figured you would want something more manly." She took a bite. Tasting his food earlier, she knew how good it would be.

Calum took another sip of wine. He regretted not bringing the bottle back with him. "Look, it may not seem like it, but I want to help you. But you can't destroy my sanity in the meantime. And you can't whisk away my best server to boot!"

Tressa put down her fork, ready to justify herself and Maggie. But Callum put his hand up almost over her mouth and shoved the glass of wine into her hand, "Just drink and shut up. We've got to last four days. Do you think you can handle that? Four days of doing things my way in my pub. It's a fair trade to get you back to your precious motherland."

Tressa snorted. "I don't have a motherland, thank you very much. Not one I want to claim as mine, anyway. Yes, I can do things your way. Just stop being mean and yelling at Maggie and me."

"I didn't yell."

"Liar." Tressa took another bite and another sip. She hated to admit it, but Callum was quite the chef. He could work as a chef in a world-class restaurant. His food was just that good.

Callum ignored her comment. "And I'll stop being mean if you stop being a pain in my ass."

Tressa sighed. "Why the hell are you helping me? You *say* you want to, but your body language and your actions scream something different. Callum, I don't want to be an albatross.

I'm an adult, and I can figure out something on my own. I'll stop being a pain in your ass permanently if you'll just point me towards a hotel." She was sick of this. Sick of him, sick of this day, sick of feeling this way. She wanted the feeling back she had at the make-up counter at McGreggor's. She wanted to feel in charge of something in her life again.

Callum stood and began pacing as he ran his hands through his hair in frustration. "Why the hell can't you just say thank you and let me help you for fuck's sake already! I - you just -" Callum scooped Tressa up in his arms and planted a kiss square on her lips. It was a kiss of frustration, energy, and a dash of lust. It was familiar to him, at least to his subconscious.

As Helen and Pat had suspected, Callum had been on the Isle only four weeks prior. It was quiet there, and he liked to visit when time allowed to write poetry or read a good book. It was his way of decompressing from running the pub. On his last visit, he had fallen asleep while reading. And now the lips he was kissing seemed so familiar it made his brain short circuit.

His lips felt soft against hers, wanting. She let out a soft sigh as she opened her mouth to him. Her tongue met his. He moved his muscular arm around her waist, pulling her closer. He put his hand on the back of her neck, massaging it as he deepened the kiss. Then, as if a bell rang, the spell broke. Breaking away from Tressa, Callum took a step back.

"Oh shit! I am sorry, I don't know what came over me. I'm not that person. Please don't think I want or expect anything to help you. I - "

Tress grabbed his hand. She wasn't sure what she was feeling, but she knew he wasn't taking advantage of her or expecting any kind of sexual recompense. "It's okay. It's really okay."

Callum grabbed his glass and sat back down behind his desk. He needed a physical barrier between himself and Tressa. "I have some paperwork I need to catch up on before I go back out there. Please tell Maggie I'll be out there soon. Your first shift starts tomorrow at eleven AM sharp." He grabbed a scrap of paper and a pen to write with. "Here are my cell and my house numbers. If you need anything before I come in tomorrow, just call me. Oh, and just leave your dishes in the sink. I'll take care of them in the morning." He turned to his computer. He was clearly done with the conversation for the evening. Tressa got up, taking her plate and glass with her. Callum looked up at her as she walked away. "Have a good night Tressa. I'll see you in the morning."

Tressa headed to the kitchen, dropping off her dishes. The bartender capped off her wine for her before she headed upstairs. She sat on her bed as she touched her fingertip to her lips and replayed what had just happened in her head. What *had* just happened? And why was her skin tingly and her insides warm? And why was thinking of Callum fumbling and nervous, making her smile? So many thoughts weaved through her mind as she got ready for bed. Once comfortable, she took out her sketch pad and started drawing Callum with the loose curl over his left eye. Tressa wondered how weird tomorrow would be, thinking nothing could top today.

~ Day Two ~

The day went by quickly. Much to Callum's surprise, Tressa was an excellent server, and the customers loved her, especially the locals. She fit into the community like she belonged there. Callum tried to keep the thought from his head. He would drive her to Dublin in a couple of days, sending her home and out of his hair. He had kept his distance since the kiss last night. But it did not stop his brain from dreaming about kissing her again. However, he stayed in complete control. Even when their arms brushed against each other in passing. Or when they reached for the same glass, letting their fingers linger just a moment longer than necessary. He only had to last two or three more days, tops.

Tressa was getting used to Callum. He wasn't really an asshole. Well, not all the time. He had agreed to let her work more than just the lunch shift once he saw how capable a server she was. She snuck several looks at him when he was interacting with customers. He laughed often, and she loved the sound of it. And when he really laughed, a full belly laugh, he would get this twinkle in his left eye. It was like a little piece of joy was sparking off into the world from that spot. She sometimes let her thoughts wander to his soft lips and dreamed about kissing them again. Although he was tall and what some would consider lanky, Tressa bit her lip, watching his muscular arms flex as he lifted kegs and crates of glass mugs. She wanted those arms wrapped around her, engulfing her, caressing her. Still, she tried to stay in control of her thoughts, keep it all professional. She had to last two, three days tops.

~ **Day Three** ~

On the third day, Tressa woke up to the smell of bacon and pancakes. Turning on her side, she saw the clock read 7:16 am. She had always been an early riser. It never occurred to her that Callum would be there so early. He'd said all meals came with her employment, and he had kept to his word. Picking a new outfit from her shopping trip, laid it on the bed before heading to the bathroom to shower and get ready to start the day.

Twenty minutes later, Callum bounded up the stairs, whistling as he went down the hall. Breakfast was ready, and he didn't want it to get cold. He hoped Tressa would at least be awake. There was an extra spring in his step, and Callum had to admit to himself it was because of Tressa. It was also because of Tressa that he was making elaborate breakfasts and trying new menu items. Two days and this woman had turned his world sideways. She was *taking the grump out of him* as his sister Mags had teased the other night.

He turned the corner just in time to see Tressa coming out of the bathroom in nothing but a towel, hair up, beads of water still dripping down her neck. She didn't see him. A couple of braids had escaped and were resting behind her ear. Scooped up by Tressa, no doubt when they fell in her face. The short towel covered her, but showed enough to make Callum want to see more.

He sucked in his breath, licking his lips as his eyes traveled down her body. He stopped to look at her luscious, round ass. It was big and beautiful, just like he liked them. He bit his bottom lip, thinking of how it would feel in his hands, kneading her ass as he kissed down her neck. A small part of him hoped her towel would drop. He could feel his manhood twitch and harden. He turned around and went down several steps to calm himself. Once he felt composed, he stomped up the stairs, signaling his arrival.

"Hey Tressa," he half yelled. He walked up to her bedroom door and knocked on it.

"Just a minute," Tressa called from behind the door. A moment later, she opened it, dressed and smiling. "Is that bacon I smelled earlier?"

Callum nodded. "Bacon, pancakes, some mixed fruit, and coffee or tea."

"Why, Callum O'Rourke, are you trying to spoil me with your amazing cooking?" Tressa smiled. *Why am I flirting with him?* She needed to change her tone. "I - Thank you. I - I'll be down in just a minute."

Callum nodded. "Of course. I'll see you in a few." He walked away as Tressa closed the door.

Tressa didn't make it to the kitchen. Callum had set out a buffet spread on the bar and had taken the chairs down at one table, complete with orange juice already poured. She made herself a plate and sat down. Callum made a plate as well and joined her.

"Thanks again for this." Tressa pointed at the spread.

Callum shrugged. "All in a day's work."

"Speaking of a day's work. Why a pub?"

Callum shrugged again. "Family business. My great grandfather started it, then my grandfather took it over, then my dad, and about six years ago it was my turn."

"You make it sound like it's not what you wanted to do."

Callum gave a shy smile as he shrugged. "It was close enough. It came down to me taking it over or the possibility of it closing, or worse, being sold."

"Sounds like you are a wonderful son. Any brothers or sisters?"

"Ha! You seem to have become fast friends with one already. Maggie is my half-sister."

"Ah! That explains why you are so hard on her."

Callum bristled, getting a little defensive. "I do NOT -"

Tressa raised an eyebrow.

Callum laughed. "Fine, I'm hard on her. But she needs it."

Tressa looked at him for a moment, waiting for him to elaborate. When he didn't, she changed the subject. "So, do you get a lot of business from the cruise ships?"

"More and more. It's been great for us. And I've never said it, but I'm sorry about you getting stuck here."

"It's my fault. I should've paid more attention. Or just taken one of the scheduled tours." She sighed. "But I'm kinda glad it happened." Tressa looked around the place. "If I had taken some boring old tour, I never would have met Maggie, Helen, or Pat." Tressa looked Callum dead in the eyes. "Or you." She held his gaze for a moment before hiding her face behind her coffee mug as she took a slow, long sip.

I'm not crazy, am I, but I think she is flirting with me? Should I flirt back? No, I should just play it cool, right? Yes, play it cool.

Callum discussed with himself in the time's span it took Tressa to drink her coffee. "Have you seen much of Cork?"

Tressa smiled. "A bit here and there. Maggie has been a wonderful tour guide. It's so beautiful here. I've gotten to do several portraits of local spots."

"Oh! You're an artist. I didn't know that. I'd love to see your work sometime. If you don't mind sharing it."

A surprised smile sped across Tressa's face. She hadn't pegged Callum for an art lover. "Sure, let me get my sketchbook before I lose my nerve." Tressa wiped her mouth and scampered upstairs.

Callum watched her go as he took a bite of his pancake stack. He couldn't help but smile, watching her ass as she left.

She came back rather quickly and handed the book to Callum.

Before opening it, Callum asked, "Did you get in touch with the cruise line?"

Tressa sighed, nodding her head. "They were as helpful as a wet bag of rocks. But they will place my things in port storage when the ship returns to the point of departure. I can pick it up from there, fingers crossed."

"It's progress though." Callum looked down at his plate. He took one more bite and then pushed it aside, wiped his hands, and opened Tressa's sketch book. He was silent as he looked through the book.

Tressa held her breath as he turned each page. Sometimes he would turn back to one he had already looked at. He looked up at Tressa "Cork City Gaol. You capture it exactly. This is wonderful."

Tressa was proud of her work. "It's the prettiest women's prison I've ever seen." She chuckled.

"Oh? Seen many, have you?"

Tressa laughed. "This was my first. I usually use watercolors, but I left them on the ship. Just brought my colored pencils."

Callum closed the book. He saw the sketch she had made of him, but he said nothing. It made him swallow hard. She had seen something in him and had translated onto the paper. Something he thought had left him long ago, pure joy. "These are fantastic. Have you had a show? I assume you sell them."

Tressa blushed and took the book back. "Thank you. I'm working on having a show someday. Right now, they're just for me. They aren't ready or good enough."

"Oh trust me, love, they are truly good enough."

I might regret this, but what the hell? He thought to himself. "Can I take you someplace today?"

"I - what about the pub?" Tressa felt like her heart was beating out of her chest. She was sure Callum could hear it.

Callum shrugged. "We're not open until noon today. No ships are coming into port. Maggie can watch the place until we get back. Besides, Betty and Siobhan are scheduled as well. Plenty of help on a no-port day. We'll return before it gets too crazy tonight. Besides, what I have in mind might give you some great inspiration. Let me show you." Callum wanted to spend time with her, just him and her. He didn't want to fight the feelings he was having. Even though she'd be leaving soon.

Tressa wanted to go wherever Callum wanted to take her. She tried not to smile or act too excited. But her stomach was doing flips. "I'd love to go. Am I dressed all right?" Tressa stood up.

Callum looked her up and down, fighting not to lick his lips. She was wearing denim shorts and a white halter top with daisies on the strap corners. Her hair was half up and half down. And she had white sneakers on. "You look perfect."

Tressa smiled. "Let me just get my bag" She headed back upstairs.

"Don't forget your pencils!" Callum called after her. He hurried to clean up. Then made a picnic lunch to take with them.

~ The Gardens ~

An hour and a half later, *Glenview Gardens & Fairy Trails* was more than Tressa could have dreamed of. She felt the Irish magic as soon as they pulled up to the place. Three acres of ten different gardens, fairy trails, plus hobbit lane. It was better than any tour a cruise ship offered. Although it was early, there were plenty of families enjoying the gardens.

Tressa and Callum were walking through the Heather Garden when Tressa suddenly came to a stop. In the center of a ring of heather stood a statue of a beautiful tree root. This is what she wanted to draw. There weren't any benches, so she sat on the ground at the side of the path so others could still walk by. She said nothing but began her work.

Tressa made fast progress, not wanting to linger, so there was time to see the rest of the gardens. All the while, Callum just stared at her, watching Tressa in her element, letting her creativity flow. So happy, so serene, and downright beautiful. It only took her about twenty minutes to capture the essence of how the tree made her feel with the colored pencils she had brought. Much cleaner and easier than her normal water colors. She handed the sketchbook to Callum. "What do you think?"

Callum looked at the picture for a minute in silence and smiled. He put his hand out to help her up. Using his powerful arms, he pulled Tressa close to him. "It's a beautiful picture. Almost as beautiful as the person who created it."

Tressa looked from Callum's eyes to his lips and back again. She gulped, trying to force air into her lungs. *I'm leaving in a couple of days. I shouldn't do anything I would regret. No, I'm leaving in a couple of days. I should do everything my heart desires.* Tressa snaked her hand behind Callum's neck, drawing him closer. She pressed her lips against his, softly at first and then with more pressure, more desire. The heather garden melted away for the both of them as Callum deepened the kiss, opening his mouth to her and demanding she do the same. Better than the first. This kiss was full of pent up longing, desire, and lust.

They came crashing back to reality with the sound of children giggling. Callum pulled away, red in the face. "Maybe we should move along? Go back to the pub? To your room?" He had a mischievous twinkle in his eye.

Tressa had more control than he did. She wasn't sure when she would be back in Cork again. "I want to see the rest of the gardens. Is that alright?" She felt like she was finding herself again, finding her heart after so many years of closing it off to keep it safe. It bewildered her, feeling like she could start opening up to someone in another country that she would leave shortly.

Callum squeezed her hand and then kept holding it. "Of course."

The rest of the day felt like a beautiful dream. Hands together, laughing and snapping pictures on Callum's phone. It was the first time in a long time that Callum let himself unwind, not worrying about every little thing. He felt light and happy. A feeling that he had almost forgotten.

As Callum parked his car in the pub parking lot, he turned to Tressa. "Today was a great day. Thank you for trusting me." He leaned in and kissed her, wishing he didn't have to go into the pub and work the rest of the night. All he wanted to do was take Tressa to bed and make her scream his name over and over. Then one more time for good measure. But he had responsibilities and the dream day had ended.

"Penny for your thoughts?" Tressa rubbed her thumb over Callum's hand.

"I just wish the pub was closed for the night already." Callum winked. "I - "

Maggie interrupted him, knocking on the car window. "What's taking you two so long? I need your help. We're in the weeds, and the band you hired is late!"

Callum groaned as he rolled his eyes. "No rest for the wicked." Getting out of the car, he went around to open Tressa's door. But she'd already opened it and was getting out.

"I need ten minutes to change my clothes, then I'll be right down to help you, Maggie." She gave Callum's hand a squeeze and headed inside.

Maggie leaned against the car with a Cheshire grin on her face. "So, you two had a good afternoon, I take it? Maybe a smooch or two?" Maggie made a kissing noise and laughed.

"Real mature, Mags."

"I'm the baby of the family. You're supposed to be the mature one." She smiled. "So, did you kiss her? I know you like her. She's good for you, but time is short!"

"I have a pub to run, if you'll excuse me." Callum headed inside.

"No answer is the same as a yes!" Maggie yelled. She loved teasing her brother. And she loved seeing him happy even more. Sighing, she headed back inside. She didn't have the heart to tell him the Embassy had opened early. She'd wait until closing.

The band arrived, and the rest of the night went well. Maggie and Tressa finished up their side work. Callum paid the band and helped them take the last of their equipment out to their van. He came back in, taking the till from the bar, and headed to the back office.

Maggie followed him. She knocked as she walked in, closing the door behind her. "I have some news."

Callum stopped counting the nightly deposit. "Oh?"

"The Embassy, it's open again. First time the government does things early." Maggie snorted.

"Oh." Callum went back to counting.

Maggie waited for him to say something. She sat and waited, and waited some more.

Sighing, he looked up at her. "I'm about done here. Mags, you can head home. But, I'm going to need you to run the place tomorrow, open to close. I promised I would take Tressa to the Embassy as soon as it opened. God only knows how long the paperwork will take."

"Cal I -"

Callum cut her off. "It's fine Mags, it's all fine." He turned his chair around to open the safe. "Have a great night, Mags. Thanks for covering for me this afternoon."

Maggie stood there for a moment. Not knowing what to say, she left. She stopped on her way out to see Tressa. "Hey Tressa, the embassy is open. Cal plans on taking you tomorrow. Maybe we could have a goodbye breakfast?"

"Oh, that's earlier than expected." She looked down, not wanting Maggie to see her disappointment.

"Plans can change, can't they? I'll see you in the morning." She gave Tressa a hug and walked out the door.

Tressa wasn't sure what to do. She thought about going into the office or heading upstairs. She went to the bar instead. Maybe it was better that things hadn't gone too far. Maybe it was time to get back to reality. So why did she feel so sad?

~ Making a Memory ~

Tressa poured herself a shot from behind the bar. Tressa decided she didn't want to mope or have any regrets. She wanted a wonderful memory. She marched herself into Callum's office. Callum, sitting in his chair, was staring off into space with a drink in hand and a bottle on the desk. She slid between the desk and his chair, leaning on the desk. "Hey."

"Hey."

"Maggie told me the embassy was open."

"Aye, it is. And as promised, I will drive you first thing in the morning."

Tressa took a swing from the bottle. "Tomorrow is later. Tonight is right now." She leaned over and started unbuttoning his shirt as she looked into his eyes. She smiled at his shocked expression on his face.

Callum grabbed Tressa's wrists. "What are you doing?"

"Do you want me to stop?" She tried to kiss his chest, but he held her at bay.

Callum looked into Tressa's eyes, searching for what he wasn't sure. But what he saw was enough. With a strength Tressa was not aware Callum had. He got up, pushed his chair aside and swung her around, pinning her up against the wall. He kissed her hard. Demanding submission. She willingly gave it, moaning as his tongue entered her mouth, taking it over. Their tongues tangoed as he pushed his hands under her shirt, caressing every bare inch he could find. Biting her lip, he kissed down her jaw to her neck. He sucked and nipped on it before biting her with a little heat behind it. "Be a good girl and keep your hands right where I have them."

Tressa's moans were his affirmation. Callum pulled her shirt over her head. He kissed across her collarbone as he undid her bra, discarding it on the floor. He cupped her right breast and swirled his tongue around her peak. She arched her back in response as he blew on it, before giving it a suck.

Tressa's breath grew raspy as he sucked and swirled her nipple. Moving over, he repeated his actions on the other. He kissed down her belly as he unzipped her jeans. Then Callum got on his knees, pulling her jeans down. As she stepped out of the pants, he cared for her legs, making sure she kept her balance. He kissed up one soft thigh and then over to the other, hovering over her sweetness, letting his hot breath saturate her. Taking his time, Callum slid her panties to the side. They were soaking wet. He smiled, knowing he was the one who had made them that way.

Callum skimmed his tongue up her folds. She gasped, bucking her hips, wanting more of his mouth on her.

"Mmm, delicious." He chuckled as stood up, pulling Tressa's jeans up with him. "Come with me. I want to do this proper like, taste more of the deliciousness." Callum grabbed her hand and led her upstairs to her room.

Once in her room, he laid her on the bed. He kissed her once more before standing up and taking off his shirt and pants.

Tressa raised an eyebrow. "Do you always go commando?"

"More often than not." He winked as he climbed onto the center of the bed next to her.

Callum wanted to take his time. He kissed every inch of Tressa's body, starting at her head, down to her toes. He dipped just a touch of his tongue into the skin with each kiss.

Tressa felt like each kiss was a mini shock of ecstasy running through her body. She bit her lip to stop herself from moaning too loudly.

Callum could tell she was holding back. "Let it out, love. I want to hear what I do to you." He took his hand and rested it in her nest of curls and applied pressure, rotating his palm. With his free hand, he rolled one of her nipples, giving it a soft squeeze before rolling it again. All the while kissing her round, luscious belly. He grabbed her body, rolling her on top of him and kissing her. Callum grabbed her soft ass, giving it a squeeze as he kissed her again. "May I give you something to remember me by?"

Tressa nodded.

Callum rolled Tressa over onto her back. He kissed down her body again, relishing in her softness, not able to get enough of her. He spread her legs, nuzzling them as he did. Callum opened her lips with his tongue, seeking her jewel. He easily found it and began playing.

Tressa whimpered at his touch. Callum put his arms around her hips, forcing her closer to his face. He enjoyed the noises he was eliciting. Her pleasure was undeniable.

Tressa moaned and cooed, never quite able to catch her breath. Others had gone down on her before, but Callum had a way that made her toes curl and her breath catch in her throat. She could feel her legs quiver. She was close, so close.

Callum circled her core with his tongue a few more times before sucking on it, bringing Tressa over the edge. She screamed out as she came, arching her back, throwing her head to the side.

Callum kissed her as the waves of orgasm subsided. He caressed her body as he made his way back to her face. He loved all the curves, mounds, and divots his hands careened over. Her skin was so supple, he never wanted to let go.

Tressa turned to her side, looking at Callum. She let her hands roam his muscular chest, taut and sweaty. Moving her hands along every line of his six-pack, she could feel his skin tingle and flinch. As she kissed him, she could taste herself on him. Kissing him was magic to her. Tressa felt like she was floating, never wanting to come down. She found his rock hard cock and began stroking it. Long stroke, slow and soft at first, then applying a little more pressure.

He groaned and licked her neck as his hand moved to her entrance and slid two fingers into her. She was so slick, quickly swallowing them within her. He curled his fingers as his palm applied pressure to her clit.

"Oh, fuck!" Tressa moaned as she gripped his shaft tighter.

He removed his fingers. "Gentle love, I've got more planned for you." Callum put his hand over Tressa's and eased it off his cock.

She pouted, lower lip out, enticing Callum to bite it. Tressa kissed his neck. "But I want to pleasure you, to please you."

Callum looked into her eyes as he caressed her cheek. "You are Tressa, I promise you are."

Tressa ran her hand through Callum's hair. "Please," she whispered. "I want to feel you inside me."

"As you wish, but just one moment." Callum got up and ran to the bathroom. He always kept some condoms in the medicine cabinet above the sink. Returning to the room, he kissed Tressa one more time before putting one on.

Tressa pulled him down. "I want you." She gasped. "I want to feel you. I want to scream your name."

Callum gave a devilish smile as he opened her thighs wider, placing his throbbing cock at her opening. "I can't say no to you." He moved in slowly and deliberately, wanting to feel every inch being enveloped within her walls. Callum groaned, and Tressa purred.

He groaned her tightness, which only made him harder. He was a little larger than she was used to, but he took his time stretching her wide.

Callum kissed her as he thrust slowly at first, but then with more speed. Tressa met his thrusts with her hips, allowing him to go even deeper. Her eyes fluttered as she gasped for breath, her whole body ablaze.

Tressa felt tingles with every thrust. Callum was almost primal, sensual and thunderous at the same time. She squeezed her walls, making a tighter grip on his rod. He growled in her ear at the sensation. "Yes, baby, take me in, hold me tight."

Tressa took him literally and dug her nails into his back. Both on the brink of pleasure. She screamed out his name as she released, digging her nails a little deeper. It only made him thrust harder as he exploded a moment after her.

Discarding the condom, he scooped her up in his arms and kissed her before grabbing a blanket to cover them both as he held her close.

Callum held Tressa through the night until the sun peeked through the curtain. Callum had his share of lovers, but no one came close to what he shared with her that night. He wanted to explore what this could be, but he knew he had to drive her to the Embassy and he didn't want to impede whatever her life plans may be. Sighing, he had to accept the moments he had with Tressa were all he was going to get, and that had to be enough. He held her a little closer, listening to her breathe.

~ The Drive ~

The sunbeams woke Tressa up. She felt Callum's muscular arms around her and smiled. This is what she imagined her life would be like. Having someone who could make her taste buds dance in the kitchen, her side stitch with laughter, and curl her toes in the bedroom. But today she was Embassy bound. She was going to get the paperwork she needed to get on a plane and fly home. Even if she wasn't sure about leaving just yet. She turned to face his chest and began kissing it. She twirled her tongue around his nipple.

Callum groaned as he smiled. "Good morning to you, too."

She slid her arm down his leg and began stroking his cock. She could feel it hardening under her touch.

"Shit, woman." He moaned. "What are you doing to me?" His hips bucked as she squeezed a little harder.

"If you have to ask, I must not be doing it right," Tressa said before she licked his nipple.

Callum growled as he flipped Tressa over so that she was on her back. "Oh love, you were doing it just right." He moved her arms above her head and held them there as he kissed down her body. Dublin was only three hours away. They had time.

Callum and Tressa came downstairs, meeting Maggie for breakfast later than planned. But Maggie didn't mind. From the noises she heard, it was a valid reason. She was glad they had gotten together, even if it was the night before Tressa was leaving.

Callum was the cook in the family. Maggie brought take out from a place in town. Callum took one look at it and shook his head. "Treason, in my own pub, throw that garbage away. I'm cooking." Thirty minutes later, Callum had set out a spread much like he had every day since Tressa arrived. And this one included his special occasion, world famous, Bailey's French toast.

They ate in silence for the better part of the meal. When they finished, Maggie handed Tressa a little bag. "Here, just something to remember us by."

"Oh Maggie, you didn't have to do that."

Maggie smiled. "I know, but I wanted to. Open it."

Tressa opened the bag to find a small box. Inside, she found a four-leaf clover pendant on a chain. Tressa looked at Maggie, trying not to cry.

"So you'll always have a bit of the Irish luck with you." Maggie smiled.

Tressa gave Maggie a hug. "Thank you, I love it!"

Callum started clearing the table. "We should get going. Don't want to get caught in morning traffic."

Maggie grasped his hand and gave it a reassuring squeeze. "I'll clean up. You go ahead." She gave Tressa a long, hard hug goodbye, making Tressa promise to keep in touch.

They filled the car ride to the embassy with music, not talking for the first hour. Eventually, Callum turned the music down. "So? What's your plan? Get your paperwork, book a flight for later today? Do you need money for a ticket?"

Tressa shook her head, trying to look upbeat. "Thank you, but I made decent money at the pub. I'm good." There was more silence. Tressa watched the scenery go by. She took a deep breath, saying what was on her mind. She looked at Callum. "Can I tell you a secret?"

Callum gave her a side glance. "Your secret is safe with me."

"When I was on the Isles, I fell asleep, and you kissed me in my dreams. That's why I missed my ship. I was sleeping, dreaming of you.

Callum raised an eyebrow, trying to keep his voice level. "Oh? Was I a good kisser?"

Tressa punched his arm. "You know you are."

Callum shrugged. "Well, dream kissing and real kissing can be very different. I had to make sure I was living up to the dream." He gave her a wink.

"So, I'm thinking I might stay a while longer. You know, through the summer. I mean, if that's okay with you. You know, staying above the pub?"

Callum pulled the car over and turned off the ignition. "Are you serious? You want to stay?"

"I - I want to explore Ireland. Explore us, if that's something you'd want to -"

Callum cut her off with a kiss. "I want you to stay as long as you want." He kissed her again. "Can I tell you a secret?"

Tressa nodded, hoping the secret was what she thought it was.

"I dreamed of you, too, about a month before you even stepped foot in Ireland. Don't you dare tell Helen and Pat, or I'll never live it down!" He kissed her again, caressing her neck as he pulled her as close as the seat belt would allow.

"I still need to go to the embassy. I need help with an ID and whatever else I need to prove I'm me for whenever I decide to get on a plane."

Callum kissed her again, with more passion and love than either of them thought possible. Then he kissed her again, this time softly. He stroked her cheek. "I guess we are stuck with you, then. Miss Tressa, the former prickly princess who has become our accidental resident."

Don't miss out!

Visit the website below and you can sign up to receive emails whenever Ruby Dare publishes a new book. There's no charge and no obligation.

https://books2read.com/r/B-A-NMGW-JXXHC

BOOKS 2 READ

Connecting independent readers to independent writers.

Did you love *Accidental Resident*? Then you should read *Covenant*[1] by Ruby Dare!

[2]

So must it be, so shall it be

His love is not an act. His humanity however.....now that's a different story.

Caolon Chain has been in and out of the entertainment magazines since his acting career began. Always an enigma, never revealing too much. Now that he's gotten his first leading role in a Broadway play he's ready to put his plan in motion. He needs to find a human bride. Someone to be his queen and rule by his side in his realm.

---

1. https://books2read.com/u/3GVp8L

2. https://books2read.com/u/3GVp8L

When best friends Runne and Shelby with a penchant for the supernatural come to the big apple on vacation they weren't expecting to come face to face with the one and only Caolon Chain. But now that they have, everything has changed.

One of them had fallen hard and fast for Caolon. The other is inexplicably drawn to him, but feels he's hiding something she can't put her finger on. Will Caolon unwittingly destroy a friendship in courting his queen? Or is something more sinister lurking on the horizon?

Covenant is the first spicy paranormal romance in the urban fantasy Fae vs. Warlock Series

About the Author

Ruby Dare is a sassy, fat, black New England woman. A writer of paranormal romance as well as contemporary romance and fantasy romance, all with one thing in common - SPICE. After studying English and creative writing in college in New York, she has lived up and down the East coast and even tried out the west coast for a couple of years. Loving the hot weather, but too far from family, she has now planted her roots in beautiful Greenville, South Carolina. That is until the romance winds whisk her somewhere new.

Follow Ruby to find out about all of her upcoming projects:
TikTok: @RubyDare
Instagram: Writergurl73
Facebook:RomanceAuthorRubyDare